Bella
dancerella™

At the Fair

5

Written by
Poppy Rose

ABC
Books

Illustrated by
Omar Aranda

'Dance-a-doodle-doo!'

'Thanks for the wake-up call, Galileo,' Bella said as she leant out her bedroom window and looked at the sky. 'The rain has finally gone.'

'It's a fine day,' crowed Galileo.

'It's fair day!' Bella cried. 'And we're all going to town! I'll be down to get the animals ready in two leaps and a ballet twirl.'

Bella opened her wardrobe door. 'I wish I could get dressed for the parade now, Roy,' she said, reaching for her purple fairy ballet costume.
'I love this costume to bits and I get to wear Mum's lucky white ribbon that we found in the attic chest.'

'And you'll be dancing at the front of Miss Tweedle's ballet float, leading the parade!' woofed Roy.

'Well, not quite at the front,' Bella sighed. 'Charlotte will be at the very front and I'll be to the side, just behind her. We'll be a magical triangle of dancing fairy ballerinas turning around in a jewellery box float!'

'It will be the prettiest float in the whole parade,' woofed Roy.

'And I've entered the baking contest for the first time this year!' Bella said.

'Your cupcakes looked amazing,' woofed Roy. 'But right now you need to get dressed for the barn. All the animals are in contests or exhibitions this year, and they're very excited.'

'They sure are,' Bella agreed.

'I hope I win the sheep-rounding contest again,' woofed Roy, bounding down the stairs.

'You've practised hard enough to win,' Bella called, skipping after him. 'I'll just put my costumes in the truck first. Today's going to be the **best** day!'

Out in the barn, the animals were eager to get ready.

'Hold still, Jasper,' Bella cried as she tied a red ribbon around his tail.

'I'm going to be so fluffy,' quacked Puddles as he gave his feathers a wash.

'And I'm so soft and white,' honked Waddles as he flapped his wings dry.

'***Stop all that splashing!***' mooed Mimmee as she crouched down to let Maggie put on her shiny new bell.

'Your mum's lucky white ribbon looks pretty in your hair, Bella,' Dad called as he finished brushing Roy's coat.

'Well, thank goodness I don't need any help getting ready,' bleated Chloe as she headed towards the barn doors. 'You lot are going to make me late!'

Chloe, Roy, Agatha and her chicks,
Puddles and Waddles and the family of
mice all piled into the back of the truck.

'Off we go to the fair then!' cried Dad as he closed the door of Mimmee and Jasper's float and then climbed in next to Bella. 'Is everybody ready?'

'**YES!**' shouted a chorus of excited voices as the truck headed down the drive and out through the gates of Meadowbrook Farm.

Later that morning at the Downy Meadows District Fair, Bella and Dad watched with delight as the animals entertained the children in the farmyard nursery.

Puddles and Waddles **quacked** and honked as they led the children on a merry duck chase. Agatha clucked lovingly as her chicks were cuddled and fed. And Mimmee **mooed** happily as she was milked by a little boy.

quack
quack

honk
honk

'Should I go to the bake-off now?' asked Bella. 'It's the first time I've entered the baking contest and I don't want to miss the judging.'

'It hasn't started yet,' Dad said. 'You've got a bit of time for rides and games!'

Bella played the Laughing Clowns.

Then she threw three hoops.

She got dizzy in the teacups.

And she screamed and laughed on the Loopy-Loops.

At the baking stand, the judging was about to begin.
Bella arrived just in time to see it.

'Your ballerina cupcakes are amazing!' Annalise
cried as Bella approached the judging table.
'They must have taken you ages to decorate.'

'I'm a bit worried they won't taste very good though,' Bella confided as she watched the judge cut one up for tasting. 'But look at your Pretty Princess cake! I'm not surprised it made it into the finals. It's way too pretty to eat!'

'Oooh!' Charlotte said loudly, ignoring both of them. 'My castle cake is the best one here. Goody! I'm bound to win!'

'Good luck, everyone,' Bella whispered as the judges rang the bell to announce the winners.

'In third place,' the judge began, 'Charlotte Castle.'

Charlotte's mouth fell open in shock. 'Only third!'

'Tied for second place,' the judge continued, 'are the Pretty Princess cake and ballerina cupcakes. First prize this year for the junior bake-off goes to the Magical Unicorn.'

'Red ribbons for both of us!'

Bella squealed, giving Annalise a hug.

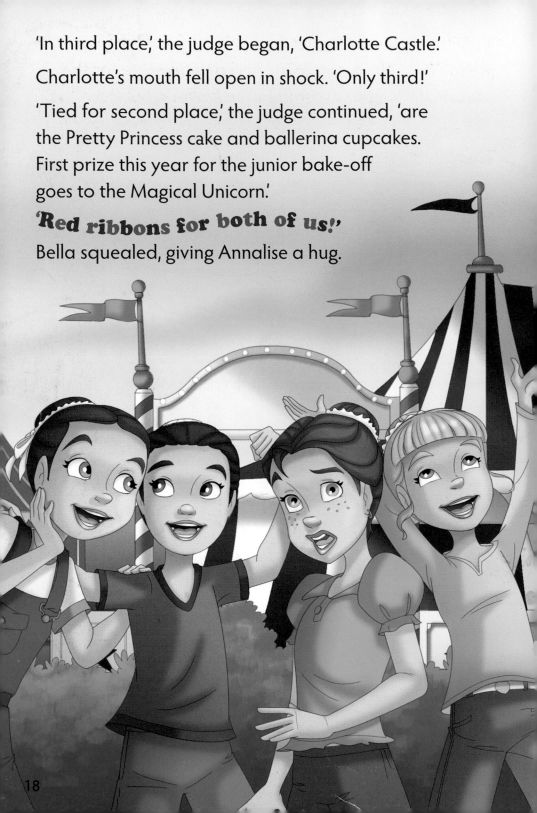

'I don't believe it,' Charlotte grumbled, snatching her green ribbon from the cake. 'And don't be late for the parade. Miss Tweedle said that a ballet scout from the State Ballet Company might be coming to check us out.'

Then she turned and walked away.

'The talent scout will be looking to see if any of us are good enough to join the State Ballet Company,' Bella said. 'That's exciting!'

'Do you think they'll pick Charlotte?' asked Annalise.

'Probably,' Bella answered. 'Hey, I have show jumping next. I'll see you later at the ballet float.'

At the junior show-jumping arena, Dad walked Jasper and Bella to the starting area. 'Second place for you at the bake-off,' he said with a proud smile. 'And a highly commended for Chloe at the gorgeous goat contest **AND** a first for Roy in the sheep-rounding event. What a trio!'

'I wish their contests hadn't been on at the same time as the bake-off,' Bella said.

'Not much we could do about it,' Dad said. 'Now, you're lucky last in this event. Are you ready?'

'Hope so!' Bella answered. She waved goodbye and led Jasper to the starting position.

The starter gun went **BOOM**, and Bella and Jasper
took off, clearing the four jumps easily.

At the last turn, Bella smiled. 'Last jump coming up,'
she said. Jasper jumped the hurdle perfectly then they
crossed the finish line to a huge cheer from the crowd.

'Congratulations to both of you on your third placing!'
Dad said as he led Jasper and Bella out of the arena
after the ribbon presentation.

'Four ribbons today for Meadowbrook Farm!' Bella cried.

'Hurrah!' Dad cheered. 'I'll take Jasper back to the
stables while you get changed into your fairy costume.
Then we'll head over to the parade floats.'

'Can we see the dog-grooming contest on the way?'
Bella asked. 'Melody's little dog, Biscuit, is in it.'

'It's pretty muddy on that side of the fields,' Dad cautioned.
'You know what Miss Tweedle said about clean costumes.'

'I'll keep my riding boots on,' Bella offered. 'I'll be fine.'

'All right, if you're sure,' Dad agreed.

At the dog-grooming entrance, large planks of wood had been laid over the mud leading into the event tent.

'At least we don't have to trudge through that mud,' Bella said, holding Roy's leash tightly as they moved into the tent.

'The judging is already over and they're about to announce the winners,' Dad said. 'We just made it!'

'In third place,' the judge began, 'Melody and Biscuit.'

'Melody looks so happy!' Bella cried, clapping for her friend.

'And second place,' the judge continued, 'goes to Charlotte and Princess.'

'Charlotte doesn't look quite so happy,' Dad observed.

'And first place is awarded to Jessica and Rocky,' announced the judge to thundering applause.

'Let's go, Bella,' Dad whispered. 'We need to beat the crowd out of this tent.'

'We sure won't beat Charlotte the way she's moving,' Bella said. 'She looks really grumpy. I guess she wanted to win badly.'

Bella, Dad and Roy ended up alongside Charlotte, Princess and Charlotte's mother on the wooden planks leading out of the tent.

'Congratulations on your second place,' Bella said.

'Thanks,' Charlotte replied shortly. 'I really wanted first place though. Looks like none of us won today.'

'Actually, Roy did!' Bella said excitedly.

GROOMING

Charlotte looked down at the beautiful blue rosette attached to Roy's collar. Then she saw the clutch of ribbons in Bella's hand. 'Move out of the way,' she snapped. 'I'm going to be late.'

Before Bella could reply, Princess lunged suddenly at Roy, causing him to rear up on his hind legs.

'Princess!' Charlotte's mother shouted as she stepped on the leash. 'Why did you let go of the leash, Charlotte?'

'I … um,' Charlotte began. Then Princess lunged again at Roy and the leash slid from under Charlotte's mother's shoe.

Bella felt something push against her and before she knew what was happening, she'd lost her balance and fallen in the mud.

Charlotte grabbed Princess's leash. Then she looked at Bella and said, 'You can't go on the float looking like that.'

'Oh, Bella,' Dad said as he helped her out of the mud.

'Take her to the basins and try to get some of the  **mud** off,' Melody's mum suggested when she saw what had happened. 'We'll let Miss Tweedle know Bella will be a bit late.'

'Thanks, but there's no point,' Bella sobbed, looking down at her fairy costume. 'No-one could clean this mess up. I don't even want to see the parade. Please can we go home, Dad?'

'My poor little fairy,' Dad said. 'Come on, let's give it a try.'

'No, Dad.' Bella sniffed. 'There's no point.'

At Miss Tweedle's float, most of the girls were in their places.

'The colours are working beautifully.' Miss Tweedle beamed as she moved around to the front of the float.

'It really is the most magical.★ float,' agreed Miss Penny. 'Thank goodness I got all the costumes made in time.'

'But where are Bella and Melody?' Miss Tweedle asked.

'The parade will start any minute. Has anyone seen them?'

'Here's Melody now,' Annalise said. 'But I haven't seen Bella since the baking contest.'

'Bella won't be coming,' Melody blurted out, a little puffed from rushing.

'Whyever not?' Miss Tweedle asked.

'She fell in the mud and her costume is totally ruined,' Melody answered. 'She's gone home.'

'Oh, what a terrible shame,' Miss Tweedle said sadly. 'And she's such a good dancer too. Well, I need someone in *purple* to move up to the second row now. Clare?'

'I couldn't, Miss Tweedle,' Clare said nervously from the back row. 'I'm not good enough to be up the front.'

'Of course you are,' Charlotte said sweetly, thinking it was a perfect choice. 'Come on, hurry up.'

'The last two rows will have three fairies each now,' Miss Tweedle said.

Just then, Bella and Dad arrived. 'Miss Tweedle,' Bella said, choking back a sob. 'I just came to say I can't dance in the parade. I'm really sorry.'

'We're off home now,' Dad added. 'Bella's very upset as you can see.'

'Oh, your hair is done so perfectly and there's not a mark on that beautiful white ribbon,' Miss Tweedle said gently.

'You know, Miss Penny does have one spare costume. Are you really sure you want to miss the parade?'

'You have another costume?' Bella asked Miss Penny.

'Only a *green* one, but it will match your eyes,' Miss Penny replied.

'And the only spot for another green fairy is in the back row,' Miss Tweedle added.

'I don't mind!' Bella jumped in. 'Honestly! Can I really still dance on the float?'

'Absolutely,' Miss Tweedle answered. 'Miss Penny will help you change. Be quick, you two. The parade is due to start!'

'Aren't you glad now that I made you come and tell Miss Tweedle you couldn't dance before we went home?' Dad asked Bella as she came back out dressed spotlessly in green.

'Thank you!' Bella answered. 'Maybe Mum's lucky ribbon is working after all. The spare costume fits perfectly!'

The jewellery box float stood
at the very front of the parade with ten still,
little fairies fast asleep atop its closed drawers.

Miss Tweedle turned the large key three times and
watched as the music began and the fairies woke.

The float moved forwards, the fairies danced and
the crowd looked on in awe.

Bella was so happy to be on the float that her beaming smile caught the eyes of everyone in the crowd, including the talent scout from the State Ballet Company.

'That little girl in green up the back is magnificent,' the scout said to Miss Penny. 'I can't take my eyes off her!'

At the end of the parade, the jewellery box music slowed and the fairies slowed with it. Then all at once the music and the fairies stopped.

Ten fairies stood perfectly still and asleep once more, and the crowd clapped and cheered loudly.

After the parade, Miss Tweedle called Bella, Annalise and Charlotte aside. 'The float was a fabulous success,' Miss Tweedle said. 'Everyone loved it. Especially Miss Lilly from the State Ballet Company.'

'She really did come and see us then,' Charlotte gasped.

'Yes', Miss Tweedle confirmed. 'And she wants the three of you to dance for her next month. Congratulations, my clever fairies!'

'This has really been the best day ever after all!' Bella squealed as she took Charlotte's and Annalise's hands and spun them round on the spot. 'YIPPEE!'